Izzie

THE CHRISTMAS
THAT ALMOST WASN'T

BUDGE WILSON

Izzie
THE CHRISTMAS
THAT ALMOST WASN'T

BUDGE WILSON

PENGUIN
CANADA

PENGUIN CANADA

Published by the Penguin Group

Penguin Books, a division of Pearson Canada, 10 Alcorn Avenue, Toronto, Ontario,
Canada M4V 3B2

Penguin Books Ltd, 80 Strand, London WC2R 0RL, England

Penguin Putnam Inc., 375 Hudson Street, New York, New York 10014, U.S.A.

Penguin Books Australia Ltd, 250 Camberwell Road, Camberwell, Victoria 3124, Australia

Penguin Books India (P) Ltd, 11, Community Centre, Panchsheel Park,
New Delhi – 110 017, India

Penguin Books (NZ) Ltd, cnr Rosedale and Airborne Roads, Albany, Auckland 1310,
New Zealand

Penguin Books (South Africa) (Pty) Ltd, 24 Sturdee Avenue, Rosebank 2196, South Africa

Penguin Books Ltd, Registered Offices: 80 Strand, London WC2R 0RL, England

DESIGN: MATTHEWS COMMUNICATIONS DESIGN INC.
MAP ILLUSTRATION: SHARON MATTHEWS
COVER ILLUSTRATION: RON LIGHTBURN
INTERIOR ILLUSTRATIONS: HEATHER COLLINS

First published, 2002

3   5   7   9   10   8   6   4   2

Manufactured in Canada

NATIONAL LIBRARY OF CANADA CATALOGUING IN PUBLICATION DATA

Wilson, Budge
Izzie : the Christmas that almost wasn't / Budge Wilson.

(Our Canadian girl)
ISBN 0-14-100272-7

1. World War, 1939-1945—Nova Scotia—Juvenile fiction.
I. Title. II. Series.

PS8595.I5813I99   2002   jC813'.54   C2002-901220-1
PZ7.W69004Iz 2002

Visit Penguin Books' website at **www.penguin.ca**

For
my dandelion friend,
Kathy Anderson

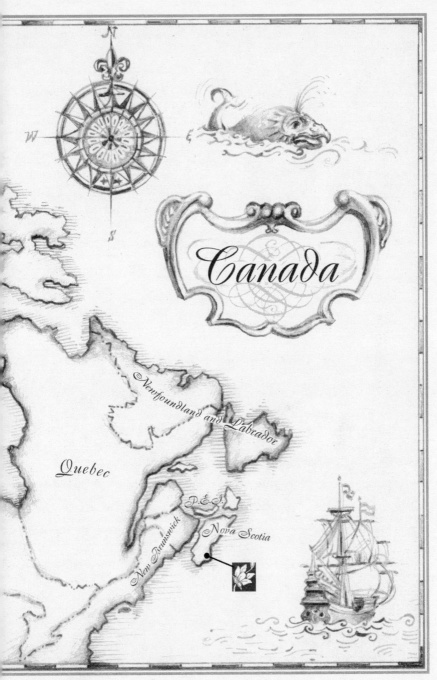

Canada

Newfoundland and Labrador

Quebec

P.E.I.

Nova Scotia

New Brunswick

 Marks the location of the story

MEET IZZIE

IZZIE PUBLICOVER LIVED IN A SMALL FISHING VILLAGE on the rugged south coast of Nova Scotia. She had a tangled mop of curly red hair, hundreds of freckles, and a lot of energy. She also wore a pair of steel rimmed glasses.

This story takes place in 1941. At that time, Canada had been at war with Nazi Germany for more than two years. Although she was only eleven years old, Izzie already knew a lot about that war.

Under Adolf Hitler, the head of the Nazi Party, Germany had taken over other countries in Europe, in order to extend its borders. Hitler had started victimizing Jews—and also Gypsies—stripping them of their jobs, moving them from their homes, taking their possessions, destroying their businesses. Eventually, these people—especially the Jews—were sent to concentration camps, where they lived under appalling conditions. Many of them died of malnutrition and illness, and ultimately millions were murdered.

Izzie also heard her parents say that Germans who openly opposed these Nazi policies were often arrested and imprisoned. She found these things scary to think about.

On September 1, 1939, Germany invaded Poland. In order to halt the actions of the Nazi government, Great Britain declared war on Germany on September 3, 1939, as did Canada on September 10. Izzie's life was never quite the same after that.

Close to Izzie's own village was the city of Halifax, which became Canada's most active wartime port. From there, service people and supplies were sent to England and Russia in convoys, which crossed the dangerous waters of the North Atlantic in all seasons.

Many of the people who lived in the small fishing villages near Halifax felt very close to the war. When they visited the city, they saw thousands of armed service personnel walking the streets, watched the convoys of ships leaving the harbour, heard the air-raid sirens practising their shrill alert. Back home, in their own communities they carefully pulled blackout curtains across their windows at night, so that enemy ships wouldn't see the lights across the water. It was Izzie's special job to do that, every night.

At that time, the people in those communities lived very simply, often with no electricity or running water. They washed their clothes on "scrub boards," made their own sauerkraut out of the cabbages they grew, got their milk and butter from their own cows, and heated their houses with logs from their woodlots. Students like Izzie often attended small, one-room schoolhouses, where all the grades were taught together.

Children as young as eleven took a lot of responsibility in those days—babysitting younger siblings, milking cows, carrying water from the well, splitting wood. By the time she was nine, Izzie knew how to milk a cow.

Without TV, sometimes without even a radio, the children of these communities learned how to make their own fun—as did their parents. There was a lot of singing and dancing, with the music made by the villagers on their own instruments. Outside the blackout curtains, it was very, very dark. But inside, the oil lamps cast a lot of warmth and light.

That's what it was like in Granite Cove, the fishing village where Izzie Publicover lived.

CHAPTER N⁰ 1

THE GREEN LANTERN

Isabel Publicover—usually called Izzie— looked out her bedroom window at the morning sea. A path of sunshine lay across the water, slightly ruffled by an early breeze.

She sighed. It looked so peaceful. But it wasn't—not really. It was 1941, and Canada was at war with Hitler's Nazi Germany. Beyond Shag Island, where the cormorants nested, she could see the far, flat horizon, sparked by a ribbon of glittering sunlight. She knew that out there— maybe right under that band of light—bad things were happening. Nazi submarines were lurking beneath the surface, searching for Canadian ships, so that they could send their deadly torpedoes into their hulls.

But Izzie wasn't going to fill up her head with gloomy thoughts. Not this morning. Today was the day when she and Joey were going to Halifax, and she could hardly wait. Joey was only seven years old—too young to have much fun with, if you happened to be eleven. She wished that Jasper could come, because he was her best friend, and almost the same age as she was. But there wasn't enough space in the truck for that many people.

Izzie had been looking forward to this trip all week, ever since her father had told them that he had to go in to Halifax to buy a special kind of twine for his lobster traps. The lobster season would start on December 1, and that was just a few days off.

"You and Joey can come with me," he'd said. "You haven't had a look at the big city in a long time. If we don't do it pretty soon, you'll forget what it looks like."

But I'll never forget, Izzie thought. She'd been nine years old the last time she'd been in Halifax, but she remembered the high buildings and big stores, the flowers and ducks in the Public Gardens, the wonderful yellow tramcars rattling along with their wicker seats and smiling conductors. And she especially remembered a big chocolate milkshake in the Green Lantern restaurant.

"Why don't we go to Halifax more often?" she asked her dad. "It isn't all that far. And they have movies there."

"Well," he answered, "with the war on, gas is rationed, and I don't like to use it just for pleasure. Besides, if the old truck wears out, I don't know where I'll find the money for another one." He looked worried—at least Izzie thought so. But Joey didn't notice. He was too young to care very much if parents worried about things. He figured they were smart enough to fix all the bad stuff. Besides, he'd just heard Izzie mention movies.

"Hey, Dad!" he yelled, grabbing him by the wrist. "Could we maybe go to a movie? Or have one of those milkshake things that Izzie keeps telling me about?"

Izzie jumped up so fast that her bright-red frizzy curls looked ready to bounce right off her head. And her round, steel-rimmed glasses actually did slide right down her nose.

"Can we? *Can we?*" she begged.

Mr. Publicover grinned. "Maybe," he said. "Maybe. If there's time. But don't count on it. I have a lot of things to do while I'm in there."

But of course they did count on it—for six days. And it was on both their minds as they climbed into the truck that morning, ready to make the trip into the city.

When they reached Halifax, after bumping along the winding dirt roads until they joined the main route into town, their father set out to do his errands. And when he finally finished all his jobs, he parked the truck in the west end of the city. Already they'd seen many groups of soldiers and sailors and air force people everywhere they'd gone, so they knew the traffic in Halifax's steep downtown streets would probably be crazy.

"We'll take a tramcar down to the Green Lantern," he said. "We'd never get a parking place anywhere near Barrington Street."

This seemed almost too good to be true. *A milkshake at a real restaurant, and a ride in a tramcar!* Izzie sighed with happiness. This was going to be even better than the last time.

But when the tram came, it was so crammed full of people that it didn't even stop. They had to wait ten more minutes for another Belt Line car. And when it opened its doors for them, they could just barely squeeze themselves in. They had to stand up all the way downtown, and they couldn't see anything but uniforms, uniforms, uniforms. They certainly couldn't sit on the funny wicker seats and look out the windows.

When they finally got off at the right stop,

Izzie could hardly believe how crowded the streets were, and she was amazed at all the many kinds of uniforms she was seeing.

"They're from lots of different countries," her father explained. "And from all over the world. This is a very big war." Izzie loved the French sailors with the red pompoms on their hats.

Between the buildings, Izzie could see the harbour, and as she watched, a long line of ships moved out to sea. It was sort of like a parade, but there was something grim and silent about it. "Not a happy parade," she said out loud.

"It's a convoy," said her father. "They're staying close together for safety. Because of torpedoes."

Izzie shivered. But she forgot about the convoy as soon as they approached the Green Lantern. Milkshakes! Something you never saw in Granite Cove. Izzie could almost taste the chocolate just by thinking about it.

But the crowded restaurant reminded them of the tramcars. You could see from the sidewalk how full it was inside, and a crowd of sailors was trying hard to push through the entrance.

"We'll never get in there," said Mr. Publicover, "and if we did, the movie would be over by the time we got served." He ducked into a drug store and came out with three ice cream cones. "Sorry, kids. But this'll have to be your supper. It's a Laurel and Hardy movie, and you'll love it. You won't even know you're hungry."

An ice cream wasn't as exciting as a milkshake, but it looked pretty good. And now the kids had their minds fixed on that magic word: *Movie!*

Izzie told herself later that she ought to have realized how it would all turn out. After all, bad things come in threes. One—squashed people in the tram. Two—no milkshake from the Green Lantern. Three? Three was staring them in the face as they got closer to the Capitol Theatre. The lineup for the movie stretched over to Salter Street, and then all the way down the hill to Hollis Street. They took their places at the end of the line, and as the people moved slowly up the hill they told themselves not to give up hope. It was 5:00 P.M. and getting colder. They stamped their feet to get warm, and Joey hugged himself, muttering, "Laurel and Hardy. Laurel and Hardy. Oh *please* let there be room for us."

But when they finally reached the ticket seller's little cage, it was 5:30—time for the movie to start. "Sorry," said the girl, with her long strip of pink tickets. "The theatre's full, and we can't take anyone else. You'd have to stand, and the company doesn't permit that."

Standing! Standing would be fine. Joey, who would have been happy to watch the movie while standing on his head, started to cry. Besides, he was cold. Inside the theatre it would have been warm.

Izzie felt like bashing the closed door of the theatre with her bare knuckles. Her father looked

Izzie told herself later that she ought to have realized how it would all turn out.

too tired and discouraged to move, but he turned in the direction of the opposite corner and said, "C'mon, kids. We can wait for a tram on the other side. Sorry. But it's not the end of the world, you know." However, he looked as though it *was* the end of the world, and he didn't make them feel one bit better. He shoved his big handkerchief at Joey and said, "Blow!"

They had to wait until two full tramcars passed them by, and when they finally got on the third they still couldn't sit down.

Later, on their way home in the truck, Izzie and Joey filled the air with their complaints about the crowded tramcars, the missed milkshakes, the closed theatre, how cold they were, how tired. Mr. Publicover said nothing. When they arrived home, he got out of the truck, went in the back door, and shot upstairs to bed without a word. He didn't even go to the outhouse before he disappeared.

Mrs. Publicover made peanut butter sandwiches for Izzie and Joey, listened to the stories about their awful day, and kept looking up the stairs towards the silent bedroom.

After a while, Izzie said, "You don't look so good, Mum. You okay?"

"I'm okay," said her mother. She picked up the oil lamp and led them upstairs to bed.

CHAPTER N.º 2

On the following morning, Izzie looked out her window, as she always did, as soon as she got out of bed. It was a clear, bright morning, but her thoughts were dark. Her mind was full of the disappointments of the day before. But she also wondered about the submarines, where they were today and what they were doing. Maybe they were looking for a chance to sneak through the giant net that protected Halifax harbour from enemy vessels.

Izzie shivered. Supposing they did get into

Halifax Harbour! They could blow up the city and the scores of ships that lay at anchor close to the docks and in Bedford Basin. Then all those thousands of people that she'd seen yesterday would be lying around on the sidewalks, wounded or dead. And Granite Cove wasn't all that far from Halifax. From the hill behind the outhouse, she could often see searchlights in the sky on a clear night, weaving back and forth, practising—learning how to pick up the shape of an enemy plane in their beams. They looked a little bit like northern lights, which she always loved to watch. But northern lights were beautiful things, shifting and sliding around in the sky. Searchlights were just plain scary.

As Izzie looked out on the peaceful bay beyond Granite Cove, she thought about the war—how sometimes you could see fiery explosions on the horizon at night; how she already knew three people who had been killed (including Jasper Morash's uncle, who had lived in Prospect); and how another man was listed as "missing." *Missing!* She hated to think of what that meant. Where was he? Was anyone looking for him?

And now—after yesterday—she knew that the war had spoiled Halifax for her. It had always seemed like such a magical place; but now it was more like a sardine can, with double the usual number of sardines in it.

Downstairs, at breakfast, Izzie and Joey did some more moaning about their day in Halifax. Suddenly, Mr. Publicover scraped his chair back from the table and said, "I'm going down to the shore to mend some lobster traps. I'll be gone all day. Make me a sandwich, will you, Bessie?" Then he went upstairs to change into his work clothes.

Izzie could see a deep crease between her mother's eyebrows as she got out the ingredients to make her husband's lunch. They always had their dinner at noon, so this was a strange thing for him to be doing. Besides, it was Sunday. Usually he just sat around the kitchen reading

The Halifax Chronicle and snoozing a bit on the couch. *A sandwich.* She made him a very big one.

That evening when the family sat down at 5:30 to their supper of weiners and sauerkraut, Izzie and Joey started grumbling again about missing the movie.

"This stupid old war!" Izzie declared. "Why does Halifax have to be so full of all those people? You can't even walk along the street without bumping into somebody. And it seems like we'll *never* get into a restaurant or a movie."

"And I've never even *tasted* a chocolate milk-shake," added Joey, talking with his mouth full of weiners, "and I've never even *once* seen a Laurel and Hardy movie."

Mr. Publicover cleared his throat and stood up.

"Listen hard, kids," he said, "because I hope I won't have to say this again."

Listen to what? Joey and Izzie hadn't often heard their father sounding so serious and stern. But he'd also acted pretty weird that morning. They stopped eating and listened.

"Those people who are filling up the Halifax sidewalks and taking up space on the tramcars just happen to be the soldiers and sailors and airmen who are defending our country. Same with the tables in the restaurants and the seats in the Capitol Theatre."

"So?" said Joey, who really didn't understand much of anything about the war.

Their father was still frowning. "So when they leave Halifax, some of them may get wounded or killed or drowned when their troopships are torpedoed. And if they manage to stay alive long enough to get to England, maybe their last happy thoughts before they go into battle will be about a chocolate milkshake or a Laurel and Hardy movie in Halifax."

"Oh," said Joey.

"So I don't want to hear any more whining," said their father. "Just decide if you want Hitler to come across the sea and invade *our* country."

Izzie stared at the sauerkraut on her plate. She'd never thought of that. She wasn't feeling very hungry any more.

Their mother didn't say anything. She just started to clear away the dishes and put them in the dishpan. It was Izzie's job to dry the dishes, so she got up from the table and got out a fresh dish towel.

Then their father went down to the shore to mend nets for an hour before bedtime. He almost never did that in the evening—especially not on Sundays—so they knew he must be really riled up.

When he was gone and the dishes were done, their mother sat down on the big rocker in the kitchen and picked up her knitting—a long, warm, navy-blue scarf for some sailor she'd never met.

The kids sat up on the couch beside the stove in the kitchen.

"He's mad," said Izzie.

"Maybe not mad," said Mrs. Publicover. "But certainly upset. *Very* upset. Everything he said is true, and I think you know that, now. But he's extra troubled because he wants to join the navy himself. He knows enough about the sea to be a wonderful sailor. But he got married late and had children late, so the government thinks he's too old to be in the war. They won't let him join up."

Izzie breathed a private sigh of relief. She'd often wondered if her father might have to go away to be part of this terrible war.

"What about Jasper's father?" Izzie was almost afraid to ask that question, because of Jasper being her best friend.

"Well," said her mother, "at the moment, the government thinks he's more useful catching fish and supporting his family than flying an airplane or learning how to fire a depth charge. Also . . ."

"Yeah?"

"Also, he's not all that young, either. And he wears glasses. Later on, they may change their minds about those things, but right now we're all more or less safe."

That night, Izzie and Joey went to bed without a story. Usually, after they got ready for bed, their father would tell them a story about what life had been like when he was a little kid. But by bedtime he still hadn't returned from the shore.

"G'night, Mum," said Izzie, as she and Joey both came over for their kiss and hug.

"Goodnight, kids," said Mrs. Publicover. Then she sighed.

"Seems to me," said Joey, when they were alone upstairs, "that Mum is doing an awful lot of sighing."

CHAPTER Nº 3

Something happened in the night, to change a whole batch of things for Izzie.

After she'd been asleep for a while, she suddenly woke up. The heat register in her bedroom was always wide open so that the warmth from the kitchen stove would reach her as soon as it was lit in the morning. Through the register, she could hear voices. Her parents were in the kitchen—maybe having a cup of the hot, strong tea they loved, before bedtime.

She heard her father say, "But I meant everything I said. They *shouldn't* complain. They've got it really easy. How would they like to be in England, where the bombs are falling?" His voice was rising.

"I know, Jeff," said her mother, keeping her own voice very low. It was hard to hear. Izzie leaned over the side of her bed so that she could listen more easily. Her head was almost on the floor. "But they're not old, like us. They're kids. It takes a while to learn things. Besides, they were pretty clobbered by what you said. I don't think they'll do any more complaining—about *those* things, anyway." Then Izzie heard her laugh.

Izzie thought she could hear a small chuckle from her father, but she wasn't sure. It was so quiet that it could have been just a noisy smile. Then her mother spoke again.

"And it's *not* always easy for our kids. They hear about bad things happening—ships going down, men they know dying, explosions out there on the horizon—lots of tragedies to worry them."

"I guess so." Her father didn't sound convinced.

"I *know* so," said her mother. "They're often sad and scared. So . . ."

"So?"

"So let's give them something really great to think about."

"Like what?"

"Like let's tell them *right now* about the special Christmas guests who are coming."

"You mean about your mother and dad coming from Yarmouth, and the Morash bunch from Sydney?"

"Yes."

Upstairs, Izzie had to bite her lip to keep from yelling. She had to hold on tight to the sheets to keep from falling right off the bed.

"But I thought we'd agreed to make all that a big surprise?" This was her father speaking.

"We did. But maybe thinking about it for almost four weeks would be even better."

"Well . . . maybe." He still didn't seem sure. Izzie guessed that he'd really liked the idea of surprising them.

But her mother wasn't finished. "Besides," she said, "I have another idea."

"Uh-oh," said her husband. "It scares me when you start having ideas."

"Well then," she said, *"just listen to this one."*

"Okay." Izzie could hear him pulling out a chair to sit down.

Her mother took a deep breath. Izzie could *hear* it.

"Let's put them in charge of the Christmas party that we've been planning with the Morashes. Jill Morash and I will do all the cooking, but they could plan everything else."

"Like?"

"Like the decorations, the entertainment, the tree, the little details that the parents always look after. Izzie and Jasper Morash can be in charge of it, and the smaller kids can help. *And we should try to keep our grown-up hands right out of it.*"

Izzie heard her father laugh. It was a good sound. "Great idea!" he said. "Trust you to make a party out of a disaster. Mind you, before we're through, we may wish you'd never had that idea. It may be a pretty weird party."

CHAPTER N° 4

The next morning, at breakfast time, Mrs. Publicover told Izzie and Joey what she and their father had decided the previous night. Izzie had to clamp her teeth together to keep from admitting that she already knew everything. She clapped her hands and made whooping noises, so that her mother would think she was surprised. It wasn't hard to look excited and pleased.

Izzie could hardly wait to get to school, so that she could tell Jasper all about it. Ideas were already jumping around in her head—about what to do and how to do it. In her brain, the tree was already cut down and trimmed, the guests had all arrived, the table was decorated, and the food was beautifully laid out on the table. She was getting on her boots in the back porch before she'd even finished her toast. As she shot out the back door, her mother yelled after her.

"Don't forget! We haven't checked this out with the Morashes yet."

"Don't worry," Izzie whispered to herself as she raced across Mr. Hyson's wharf to reach the shortcut to the schoolhouse. "They'll love the idea!"

As she rounded the corner beside the Dorey family's bark pots, she could see the school up on the hill beside the Granite Cove cemetery. It was painted orange, and in the early morning sunlight it looked almost like a doll's house, or a Monopoly house. But it didn't need to be big. There were only nineteen kids in Granite Cove—ranging in age from two to fifteen—so the school only needed seventeen desks. Jasper's little sister, Alice, and the Zwickers' baby were too young to need desks yet.

Izzie knew that in the city—in Halifax—most schools had separate rooms for each grade. And sometimes the classes were huge. She knew of one girl in the city who had sixty-six kids in her class—all in one room! The girl had told her that the teacher always seemed to be cranky. *No wonder!* thought Izzie. She'd hate to be in that room. She loved listening to the big kids' lessons, and learning about all kinds of things that weren't in the grade six readers. When she finished her work and was waiting for the teacher to get back to grade six, she'd just sit there and think about what was being taught to the grade nines or tens. Sometimes she understood, and sometimes she didn't. But it was fun trying.

It was later than Izzie had thought, so she was surprised to see Mrs. Hennessey appearing at the door with the big brass school bell. Everyone rushed inside, hung up their coats on the hooks along the wall, and lined up their boots in a row on the floor below. There wasn't going to be time to tell Jasper about the party until recess.

But she could think about it until then. She already knew that it was going to be held in her house. She'd been told way back in early November that the Morashes and Publicovers would be having Christmas dinner there. Mrs. Publicover had won not one but two big turkeys in the church raffle, and Mrs. Morash had won a basket of plum puddings and candy canes. The turkeys were waiting for Christmas in Uncle Joe's fish plant freezer in Halibut Harbour. With so much food being rationed—things like sugar, butter, meat—these prizes were going to make the dinner very special this year.

Inside the Publicovers' house was a little shop. And the party—which had suddenly become a very huge party—was going to take place there. It was a big room with four tables and a lot of shelves, but no real counter. On the shelves were bags of sugar and flour, and glass jars full of split peas and dried beans. In a corner of the floor were large crocks of sauerkraut and mincemeat made by Izzie's mother, as well as jars of her own blueberry jam and pickled beets. Piled up on the tables were various kinds of fishing supplies—nets, hooks, ropes, gaffs. On the wall was a calendar, with a picture on it of a battleship lumbering through the cold waves of the North Atlantic. The whole ship seemed to be coated with ice.

There'd be lots of room in the shop for the big party. In her head, Izzie swept all the merchandise off the tables, pushed the bags and jars into the corner, trimmed the Christmas tree, decorated the tables, watched her mother bring in the huge turkeys. She hardly noticed when Mrs. Hennessey said it was recess time. When she finally woke up and realized what was happening, she grabbed Jasper's arm and whispered, "Meet me behind the outhouse."

And it was there, behind the little outhouse— painted orange to match the school—that Izzie told Jasper about her mother's wonderful plan.

CHAPTER № 5

All week long, every time they had a free minute, Izzie and Jasper talked about Christmas. Their minds were so full of plans for the party that they didn't have time to even *think* about the war.

Jasper and Izzie had been friends ever since they'd been put in the same playpen so that their mothers could have a peaceful cup of coffee once in a while. But that was at least ten years ago. With Izzie's short, bright red curls and Jasper's jet-black hair, people said that they looked like

Hallowe'en kids—orange and black, and together most of the time. "I'm the pumpkin," Izzie would say to Jasper, "and you're the witch's black cat."

But they weren't preparing for Hallowe'en now. They were getting ready for Christmas. They had so much to do before the twenty-fifth, that it would take up all their energy and time and thinking.

One day, after school, they walked on the beach, popping rockweed bubbles and looking for sand dollars.

"What do you think is the best part of this whole Christmas thing?" asked Izzie.

"The guests!" They both yelled it out together.

"Yeah," said Izzie. "My grandparents, driving all the way from Yarmouth, and—"

"And my aunt and uncle and their three kids coming by train from Sydney." Jasper—often a serious person—couldn't stop grinning.

"And *that*," said Izzie, "is why our Christmas party has to be so perfect."

"Dad'll clear all the bags of salt and barrels of

fish bait out of his truck," said Jasper, "and drive up to the Halifax train station to collect the whole family."

"What about the gas?" said Izzie. She knew that Mr. Morash needed a lot of gas coupons, because he sold his fish along the shore.

"He says he doesn't care if he runs out," Jasper said. "He says this is more important."

Outside the Publicovers' shop, there was a tall, wide, glass cylinder that held gas. Inside the cylinder, a red liquid went slowly down as gas was pumped into your car. Then it would fill up again with a lot of wild splashing. Izzie loved to watch this happen. There weren't as many cars making that red stuff go up and down any more. But on that day, they could watch the Morashes' tank being filled.

"I bet your mum will put all sorts of pillows and blankets in the back of the truck to keep your guests warm and comfortable," said Izzie. She figured that the trip would be almost as good as a sleigh ride. There'd be plenty of room in the back for Izzie and Jasper, too. Their parents said that they were old enough to help out with the littlest kids.

Everyone would be arriving on December 24. Just thinking about the arrival of all those people made Izzie's tight red curls jiggle up and down with excitement. Behind her round glasses, she closed her eyes and thought about the food. It was hard to stop thinking about those two huge, juicy turkeys, the big plum puddings, and the candy canes. But first would come the ride in the truck.

Izzie gritted her teeth so that she could imagine that trip more clearly. She could feel the cold wind whizzing through the truck, making all of their cheeks pink. Maybe the moon would be shining down on them (she couldn't remember if it would be full), or perhaps there might be a gentle snowfall. She swept away the idea that it could be raining. Anyway, she knew they'd all be singing Christmas songs: "Silent Night"; "Hark! the Herald Angels Sing"; "Joy to the World."

Maybe one of the little kids—the baby—would start to cry. Then she'd pick him up and rock him till he was happy again. Izzie thought she'd bring a string of bells that someone had given her a long time ago. She'd shake them as they drove along, and it would be like a real sleigh ride, even if there was no horse and no sleigh—and not even any snow yet!

CHAPTER N.º 6

The next day, Jasper and Izzie held their first meeting about the party—to make plans, and to figure out who was going to do what. Jasper was babysitting his sister, Alice, and Izzie brought along her brother, Joey. Because he was seven, he could be pretty useful. Alice was three and a half. Jasper said, "I betcha she'll be more trouble than she's worth." She had hair so black that it was almost blue, and she wore it in two fat pigtails, with bangs across her forehead, almost down to her eyes.

They met in Mr. Morash's fish store, where he stored bait and rope and nets and anchors. It wasn't a store where you bought things. It was just a place for *storing* things. The only place in Granite Cove where you could *buy* things was at the Publicovers' little shop, in their house.

Jasper and Izzie had to do a lot of thinking. How many guests would be at their party? How many chairs would they need—and plates and glasses and forks and knives? Jasper sat on one of the stools, but Izzie remained standing. Joey sat up on a barrel of salt and listened. Alice cruised around the little building, picking up things and inspecting them—a long, handmade wooden needle for mending nets, a set of tide tables, a hammer, a hatchet, spools of twine.

Izzie was the first to speak.

"A meeting always has a president," she announced. "Otherwise, everyone talks all the time, and things don't get decided. I think I should be the president, because this party was my mother's idea—even though Jasper is twelve and I'm only eleven. Besides, the party's gonna be in our shop." The sun was shining in through the west window of the store, and her hair looked very, very red.

Jasper raised his eyebrows and chewed his lower lip. He said, "Well, okay, I guess. But I get to be vice-president, because we're having this meeting in my dad's fish store. And we have to prepare a lot of the stuff in here, too." Then he muttered under his breath: ". . . which should be almost as important as having the idea in the first place."

"And me?" asked Joey.

"You get to be the gofer," said Izzie. "You go for things we need and obey our instructions. A gofer is one of the most important people in an organization."

"And Alice?" grinned Jasper. She was sitting on a lobster trap, looking up at them from under her black bangs, holding a wooden box with "HOOKS" written on the lid.

Izzie laughed. "She's the one who'll get in the

way—if she doesn't get those fish hooks stuck in her fingers and wind up in a Halifax hospital."

Izzie moved over and sat down on a fish box beside the fish-cutting table, with a pad of paper on her lap and a pencil behind her ear.

"Okay," she said. "The meeting will now begin. I'll write down your suggestions."

Jasper was all ready. "We'll make a ton of popcorn and pick a lot of rosehips. We can string them together for the table. And maybe for the tree." There were enough wild rosebushes in Granite Cove to cover a football field.

"What tree?" asked Joey.

"The one I'm gonna cut down," said Izzie. "Probably the little spruce tree beside Mr. Hyson's back porch. I bet it's in his way." In Halifax, people *bought* Christmas trees. Not in Granite Cove. There was a forest behind their houses and it was made up of big and little spruce and fir trees.

"I know how to make birds out of paper," interrupted Jasper. "They're easy. Even Joey can learn how. We can put them all over the tree."

"And a big one on top," added Joey. "And what do you mean, *even* Joey can learn how?"

Jasper ignored that question. "Okay, Izzie," he said. "What else?"

Izzie looked at the ceiling so she could think better. "We'll sing a bunch of songs, and Mum can play her guitar. I just wish someone knew how to play old Uncle Herman's accordion—or that he was still alive to do it himself." Izzie felt sad for a moment. Uncle Herman—her *mother's* Uncle Herman—had lived with them ever since she could remember. But he'd taken her father's boat out last January to celebrate his ninety-third birthday. "Just to look at the bay," he'd said. But it was so cold that he'd caught pneumonia and died. Ever since then, his room had been empty and the accordion silent.

Izzie took a deep breath, and then went on. "We should have red tablecloths for the tables. Jasper and I can get some sheets out of our closets, and I'll dye them red. I know how to do it, and I know where Mum keeps her red dye. All I'll need is a big lobster pot and a lot of boiling water. I can do it some day when there's no one home, because it ought to be a surprise. And we can—"

"Hey! Wait a sec," interrupted Jasper. Izzie was fun and full of ideas, but she was definitely bossy. She liked to run the show. "Give someone else a turn. Joey, you got a suggestion?"

Joey screwed up his face and said, "My only suggestion is that someone better take that box of fish hooks away from Alice. She's got the top off."

Jasper leapt up from his chair and grabbed the box. Alice sat down on a pile of rope and looked mad. She started pulling a loose strand of wool from the leggings her mother had knit, and they began to get shorter and shorter.

Izzie couldn't wait for all these interruptions. "And we'll make decorations for the middle of the tables. Maybe with paper flowers and pipe cleaners. And we'll bring chairs from all the rooms, and milking stools from the barn for the little kids."

She jumped off her box and stood up to make her next announcement.

"It'll be our best Christmas party ever," she said, "and it'll be *really easy to do*."

CHAPTER N°. 7

Izzie had certainly meant it when she'd said that preparing for the Christmas party would be easy. But she was wrong. It wasn't easy at all. School wouldn't finish till December 21, so they had only the weekends and late afternoons for making decorations. They did most of their work in Mr. Morash's fish store, but if he needed it for mending nets or lobster traps, they had to go somewhere else, lugging all their supplies back and forth from one place to another. Sometimes they used Mr. Publicover's store, when he was up at the house, working in the shop. But it was small, and there weren't many things to sit on.

They waited and waited for one of their mothers to leave the house, so that they could make the popcorn and dye the sheets. They wanted everything to be a secret. They also thought that their mothers mightn't be all that thrilled with this part of their preparations.

Finally, Mrs. Morash got a drive into Halifax one Saturday, to buy Christmas presents. So at last they could do their biggest jobs.

Izzie had promised her mother that she'd do some ironing for her, but this was too good a chance to miss. She shoved the basket of dry laundry under the stairway and shot out the back porch.

"I'll be back!" she yelled at her mother, just before she slammed the storm door.

Soon, all the kids were gathered in the Morash kitchen, ready to work. But then, everything seemed to go a little bit crazy.

It turned out that if you filled the huge lobster pot with water, it was too heavy to carry. So Izzie had to keep filling it on the stove with the Morashes' tiny little dipper, which the family used for quick drinks of water and for filling the small washbasin in the back porch. And Jasper had to keep going out to the well for more and more water. Those buckets were heavy, and he did a lot of groaning.

Then the water took forever to boil. Izzie fed the stove over and over from the woodbox beside the stove, and everyone hoped the Morashes wouldn't notice how much wood was gone from the giant woodpile at the back door.

Alice kept going too close to the stove, and Joey had to think up ways to keep her busy and out of everyone's way. He took her into the living room to play "Giant Steps" with her, and "Piggy in the Hole" on a hooked rug, and "I

Spy." Izzie scalded the tips of two of her fingers when she was stirring the dye into the sheets, and had to dip them into the butter dish to make them feel better. When they were finished, the long wooden spoon was red, and the sheets were only pink. Then they were left with all that coloured water that they didn't know what to do with.

"And how are you gonna get the sheets dry?" asked Jasper.

Izzie bit her lip. "Don't you worry about *that!*" she snapped. She drained them in the sink until they were cool enough to handle. Then she dragged them across the kitchen floor and out into the backyard, leaving a trail of pink water behind her.

"I'm hanging them across the trees in the back woodlot," she said, as she headed for the forest.

Jasper was getting ready to make the popcorn. Just before Izzie disappeared into the woods, he yelled, "How much do I put in the pot?"

"Lots!" Izzie yelled back. "And don't forget to shake the pot. *Hard!*" Then she started to hang

She dragged them across the kitchen floor and out into the backyard, leaving a trail of pink water behind her.

the sheets over the smaller trees, to the left of the barn.

As the corn started to pop, Joey and Alice came back into the kitchen to listen to the wild pinging sounds against the sides of the metal pot. It sounded like hail on a tin roof. Then the lid started to rise, and all of a sudden the popcorn started flying all over the kitchen. Joey and Alice were shrieking with laughter, and Jasper was running to the back door to call Izzie back in.

"Hurry!" he shouted. "The kitchen's full of popcorn, and the pot smells like it's burning. *Hurry!*"

Izzie left her sheets and came rushing back into the house. Then she joined Joey and Alice in their shrieks of laughter.

"Well!" she said, when she was finally able to speak. "When I said, 'lots,' I didn't mean *that* much! But never mind. The house didn't burn down, and we've sure got lots of popcorn for the tree."

"There won't be any room for the birds on it," wailed Jasper.

Joey and Alice were scooping popcorn off the floor into big paper bags, which they kept dropping and spilling, because they were laughing so hard.

"I can't see anything to laugh about," moaned Jasper to Izzie, as he sat hunched over the kitchen table. "It's *our* pots that are full of pink water and burnt popcorn. *You* don't have to explain all that to *your* mother."

"No," agreed Izzie, hiccuping to stop laughing. "But I had to explain to my father why we used so many of his nets yesterday, to make a playpen for Alice. I told him it was a great way to keep her out of the way when we were making our paper birds and flowers in his store. And worse still . . ."

"What?" Jasper was looking more cheerful.

"It was me that Mr. Hyson bawled out when I cut down his tree. How was I supposed to know that he was using it to hide his garbage cans? Now he has to walk twice as far when he puts the garbage out. Was he ever *mad!*"

"Some party!" said Jasper. Then he made a snorting sound through his nose and started to laugh, too. "Maybe the one who'll get in the biggest trouble will be my dad."

"Why?" asked Izzie. They all wondered what he was talking about.

Jasper grinned. "Because he's the one who's supposed to be babysitting us."

It took a long time to clean up that kitchen.
Izzie found some towels in a cupboard and used
them to mop the pink water off the floor. This
made the towels both wet and dirty, with pink
splotches. So she had to wash them in icy cold
water, wring them out as tightly as she could, and
then pass them along to Jasper. He hung them up
on the clothesline by the back door.

"I sure hope my mum doesn't ask too many
questions," he mumbled, his mouth full of
clothespins.

Even with Joey and Alice stuffing popcorn into paper bags, bits of it kept escaping onto the floor and getting into the cracks between the floor-boards. And it took Jasper an hour to get the burn marks off the pot.

Out in the woods, the sheets waved around in the wind; it wasn't hard to see them if you knew where to look. They took five days to dry. Later on, the dye in the pink sheets would leak out and make everyone's pyjamas and nighties turn a different colour. None of the parents would be very pleased about *that*.

But in spite of all the setbacks and disasters, everything was ready for the party by the evening of December 21. And they still had three days before the visitors were due to arrive. The kids were so excited that every one of them, except Alice, found it hard to fall asleep that night.

In the morning, Izzie woke up much later than usual. She could see by the little clock beside her bed that it was already 8:30. Usually her father woke her up at 6:00, so that she could milk one of the cows and carry in some kindling from the woodshed. Why had nobody called her?

She opened her blackout curtains and looked through the window. Outside, she could see that dense clouds were forming across the sky, and moving very quickly. Gulls were tearing through the air as though they were being chased. They were flying low in the sky, aimed at their nests on Squid Point. The sea was an inky grey, with whitecaps racing in from the east. She'd never known it to be so dark at this time of the morning. The floorboards were icy cold beneath her feet, so she pulled on her warm wool socks before she rushed downstairs.

Her mother was in her rocking chair beside the window, doing nothing. Just sitting and looking. Mrs. Publicover was always busy—*always*. If she wasn't cooking, she was mending. If she wasn't mending, she was working in the shop. But this morning? *Nothing*. There had to be something really terrible going on.

"Mum!" yelled Izzie. "What's *wrong?* And why is it so *dark?* It gives me the creeps."

Mrs. Publicover's sad face turned away from the window. "We let you sleep," she said, "because we didn't want you to know what's happening."

Izzie was mad. She felt like stamping her foot—like Alice. "That doesn't tell me *anything*," she said.

"Listen, Izzie," said her mother, putting one arm around her shoulder, "old Mr. Gaetz says it's going to be bad."

"*What's* going to be bad?"

"The weather," sighed Mrs. Publicover. "You know how he always just *knows* what the weather is going to be like? He sort of sniffs the air, looks at the sky, and holds up a wet finger to feel the wind."

"And?" Izzie pounded the arm of the rocker. Was her mother *never* going to explain?

"And he says that what's coming could be almost as bad as the Saxby Gale. And you've heard what *that* did—way back in 1869. Ripped up wharves like they were matchsticks, and yanked a whole fish store off its posts and blew it to smithereens."

Izzie shivered in her warm nightie. She could think of only one thing.

"But they'll be able to get here, won't they? Grandma and Grandpa, and Jasper's aunt and uncle and cousins? A little wind won't stop them. Besides, they're not coming till day after tomorrow." Izzie was feeling almost all right again.

Her mother took in a long breath, and let it out slowly. "We're not talking about just a little wind, Isabel. We're talking about the biggest blow that I've ever seen in my lifetime. Mr. Gaetz just *knows.*"

Izzie spoke through her teeth. "Maybe this time he *doesn't.*" She frowned. "He could be wrong, you know." But she noticed that her mother had called her Isabel. She only did that when something important was happening.

Mrs. Publicover continued. "Sandy Jollimore has a battery radio. He says it's hard to hear what it says, but they seem to be warning people to tie things up real tight and to bring the small stuff indoors—buoys and lobster traps and other gear. And even to try to haul our boats up on land. Izzie . . ."

"Yeah?"

"Look out the window. Even Jasper is down there helping the men."

Izzie looked. It was dark, and there was a lot of spray. But it didn't look like anything that would tear the village apart. Or stop a train.

"It'll probably let up tonight," she said. "Then it'll be easy for all our visitors to get here."

"I was right to let you sleep," said her mother. "You're not even listening. Mr. Gaetz also says he can smell snow in the air. He figures that by midnight we'll be into a blizzard that might cover the whole province. With this wind, there'll be drifts that no train or car could ever get through." She stopped, but then added, "The radio says the same thing. Uncle Joe even brought the turkeys over last night that he'd been keeping in his freezer—just in case . . ."

"Well," said Izzie, forcing a laugh out of her tight chest, "what's a little snow? We've all seen *that* before. Mr. Gaetz may smell snow, but he doesn't know *how much*. Besides," she added, "there are still two more days."

Mrs. Publicover rolled her eyes. "I'll warm up your breakfast for you. Then go on up and get dressed in your warmest clothes. That big sweater that Aunt Julie sent last Christmas. Those wool leggings that I knit for you for coasting. Wind that big long scarf of yours twice around your neck and once around your coat. And tie that heavy kerchief around your head. Your stocking cap would blow off in two seconds."

"Why?" Izzie was puzzled. Why go out on a day like this?

"Because the men down there could use an extra pair of hands. They have a lot of work to do before the storm strikes."

Before the storm strikes. Izzie was quiet as she ate her porridge and toast. So this wasn't the storm. Not yet. There was worse to come.

CHAPTER N.º 9

Izzie put on her heavy clothes and opened the door. The wind was stronger now, and waves were striking the breakwater and spilling over the top. As she left the house, she could hear her mother calling—"You forgot the kerchief for your head! Come back!"—but she paid no attention. She just hoped that the wind wouldn't rip off her glasses.

She raced down to the wharf and started lugging buoys and small gear into her father's fish store. Already they'd lost a couple of wooden boxes off the stage, and these were jumping around on the sea like dumplings on top of a boiling stew.

Over by the launch, a group of men were struggling to drag a dory and a flat up onto dry land. The timbers of the launch were slippery, and Izzie winced as she watched her father almost lose his balance and slide down between them.

Mr. Gaetz was right. This wasn't just any little wind. This was shaping up to be a very, very big blow. But she couldn't see a single snowflake. Maybe he'd be wrong on *that* one. Then her grandparents and all the others could start their trips on the twenty-fourth, when the big blow was over.

In the afternoon, the wind picked up, and it was even hard to open the door to get out to the well. But when they did open the door, what they heard was a steady roar—more like the noise from a huge factory than from the wind. Everyone was inside now, because it wasn't safe for people to be down by the shore. Izzie's father had tied a strong rope onto the barn door and joined it to a nail on the house. He could hang onto that rope when he had to go out to milk the cows.

In spite of her fears, Izzie watched the storm from the window, marvelling at its beauty and destructive power. Mrs. Henkel's outhouse blew over, and Joe Murphy's small flat came loose and broke into a hundred pieces on the rocks. The waves were so high, even in the shelter of the cove, that Izzie found it hard to believe what she was seeing. It was scary, but it was also kind of wonderful.

"Hey, Mum," she asked, "is it a terrible sin to love a storm, even while it's knocking down Mrs. Henkel's outhouse and smashing up Joe Murphy's flat?"

Mrs. Publicover thought about that for a few moments. Then she spoke.

"No," she said. "I don't think so. We can't really help what we think or feel. It's not like you made the storm happen. Or told it what to do."

Izzie thought about sin. Mrs. Hennessey said it was a sin to lie or steal or to cheat on an exam. Or to hit other people. Maybe her mother was right. Maybe thinking wasn't a sin kind of thing.

All day long the storm tore through the communities up and down the coast, but still the snow didn't come. Everyone went to bed, full of hope. Maybe old Mr. Gaetz *would* be wrong, this time. Before Izzie closed her eyes, she snuffed out her oil lamp and looked out the window one more time. Just waves and thrashing trees. No snow. She smiled. Everything was going to be just fine.

Izzie woke up at about midnight when she heard a strange sound. It was like a thousand little needles striking the glass on her window. Sleet! She jumped out of bed and rushed across the cold floor to her window. But before she even reached it, the sound changed to something more muffled. Snow! It was driving against the window so hard that she couldn't see anything beyond the thousands of tiny flakes that were sticking to the glass. She crept back to bed and pulled the covers up over her head. And she wondered if Jasper was awake right now, thinking the same thing that she was thinking.

The wind kept up all night, and by morning the snowdrifts were piled more than halfway up the back door and at the entrance to the barn. Mr. Publicover had to shovel a path right around the house to clear the snow away from both doors, so that he could get in to milk the cows. He couldn't even force the back door open.

The wind was weaker now, and by noon it had calmed down to a small winter blow. But the snow didn't stop. It kept right on falling until dusk, and by then it was deeper than anything anyone had ever seen.

Izzie and Joey came into the kitchen to ask the question they'd tried not to think about all day. Izzie was the one to speak.

"Well," she began, "tell us. Stop acting like nothing's wrong. Will they come? Can the trains and cars get through all this snow? Will we be spending Christmas Day *all alone?* Will all our beautiful Christmas plans be wrecked?"

Mrs. Publicover had tears in her eyes and said nothing. She looked at her hands and her chin wobbled. So it was Izzie's father who did the talking.

"I'm sorry, kids," he said. "*Real* sorry. But no. There's no way they'll be able to get here tomorrow. There aren't enough snowploughs in the world to be able to clear away all this mess."

A *mess*. That was one of Mr. Publicover's favourite words. If a big blow tore apart the ropes on his lobster buoys, it was a mess. If two men had a big fight, it was a mess, or maybe "a racket." And certainly, this snowstorm was a *very* big mess.

CHAPTER N° 10

Christmas Eve was a sad day for the two families, although Izzie's mother tried to keep a smile on her face as she crumbled up the bread that she'd baked a week ago for the turkey dressing. And Mrs. Morash didn't even complain about using up the last of her sugar ration to make the hard sauce for the puddings. Izzie's father and Mr. Morash were outside with the other men, shovelling narrow paths through the village, so that neighbours could at least move around between their homes and barns. People from the village kept coming into the Publicover shop with ration coupons for sugar and tea. It would be closed at noon, and wouldn't be open again until December 27. And everyone seemed to have left their shopping until the very last minute.

Izzie and Jasper found two spare shovels and cleared a path from the Morash fish store to the Publicover house. This seemed to take forever, and when they had finished the job they lay down in the deep snow and huffed and puffed and made snow angels. Then, as soon as the Publicover shop closed, Joey helped them cart all their party materials up to the house.

Jasper grumbled all the way. "All this work," he moaned, "and all for nothing! What's a stupid old party without guests?"

Izzie stopped so suddenly that Joey fell flat on his face in the snow, burying a big bag of paper birds. "Look, Jasper Morash," she snapped, "you can just *stop that! You* can be *our* guests and *we* can be *yours.* That way it'll be an okay party, even if it's kind of small."

"And *ordinary*," muttered Jasper. "Just us—an ordinary Granite Cove bunch of people."

"Oh c'mon, Jasper," growled Izzie, who was struggling to keep a pink sheet from trailing in the snow. "When we get our shop all decorated up, you'll see how dumb it was to call this party *ordinary!*"

Izzie was right. By suppertime, the little shop looked as though it could have been one of Eaton's display windows. The pink tablecloths were spread across the four tables. Mrs. Publicover had pushed them all together to make a banquet table, after she'd removed all the merchandise. The tree was sitting on a wobbly stand that Jasper had nailed together, and it was so full of birds and popcorn that it was hard to find the branches. The paper flowers were stuck onto the pipe cleaners in

Robertson's marmalade crocks, and a string of rose-hips and popcorn was pinned all along the edges of the tables. Mrs. Publicover had been pretty alarmed when she'd discovered that all the pins had disappeared out of her pin box, because it wasn't all that easy to get pins during wartime. But when she saw what they'd been used for, she didn't say anything—out loud, anyway. To herself she said, "Maybe they won't all be bent when I get them back."

The kids looked at the tree, the table, the whole room, and groaned with pleasure. Jasper had even made a wreath out of spruce boughs, and hung it over the picture of the battleship on the calendar—just so they could pretend, for one day, that there was no war happening.

"It's *gorgeous!*" sighed Izzie, and Jasper agreed.

"Even though it's just us," he said, "I guess it'll be okay. And we can go coasting on Christmas Day. Mr. Gaetz says the sun is going to shine for the next two days."

"And I believe every single thing he says," grinned Izzie.

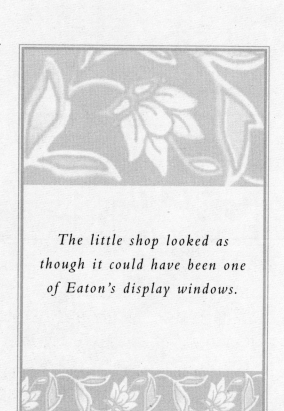

The little shop looked as though it could have been one of Eaton's display windows.

CHAPTER N° 11

The Morashes and Publicovers spent Christmas morning at their own homes, opening presents and getting ready for the big meal. They tried not to look at the left-over presents under the tree—all ready for the guests who weren't going to arrive. People in Granite Cove always had Christmas dinner at one o'clock, but they'd all decided to have the special meal at night instead of at noon, so that the kids could take their sleds and toboggans out to enjoy the snow in the afternoon. As Mrs. Publicover said to Mrs.

Morash, "The kids deserve to get something better than misery out of this big blow. Besides, we can have candles and light the oil lamps for the meal. That's a lot more like a real banquet than eating in the middle of the day."

So, by one o'clock, the kids were out on the high hill behind the Publicover outhouse, racing all the way down on the toboggan or on canvas salt bags, and then climbing up to do it all over again. From the top, they could see the whole cove below and far out to sea. They had so much fun that they almost forgot about the storm and the war and the party with no guests.

As she climbed the hill for the hundredth time that afternoon, Izzie wondered about the ships out there on the ocean. What happened when this much snow fell on the deck of a ship? Did sailors actually *shovel* it? And what about on the battlefields? Maybe they'd take a day off from fighting and just lie down and make angels in the snow. Or have a snowball fight—a whole lot better than bullets and guns. She'd heard that sometimes soldiers put away their guns on Christmas Day. Why couldn't they do that *every* day? Izzie sighed. She knew there were real reasons for this awful war. But it seemed crazy, somehow, that the only way to stop terrible things from happening was to do things that were almost as bad.

By now, Izzie was close to the top of the hill. She turned around to find out where the other kids were.

From where she stood, Izzie could see far out to sea, beyond the Seal Ledges, clear out to the horizon. Suddenly she realized that she was looking at something strange on the ocean just off Shag Island. Not a flat. Not a dory. But what? She yelled down the hill:

"Hey, kids! Get up here fast! There's something out there, and I think it's some kind of a boat. Hurry!"

By the time the other kids reached her— which took quite a while because they had to almost *drag* Alice up the hill—she could see the object more distinctly. "It *is* a boat," she said, "and it's coming this way." Sometimes it was good to wear glasses. In certain lights, you could see extra clearly.

As the boat came abreast of Squid Point, they could see that it contained at least two people. Two men were rowing, but someone else seemed to be in there, too.

"C'mon!" yelled Izzie. "If we don't get a move on, they'll reach the government wharf before we do." She flung herself down on her toboggan and went whizzing down the hill.

When they all reached the government wharf, they could see that a small crowd had already gathered. The kids weren't the only ones to have seen that strange-looking boat rowing in. Mr. Hyson was there, and so were Joe Murphy and Sandy Jollimore and Mrs. Henkel and the Knickles. Even old Mr. Gaetz had managed to hobble over to the wharf. Mrs. Publicover was running down the hill with her apron still on; you could see the lace on its hem drooping down below her coat. There were about twelve other fishermen, and lots of kids. Izzie and Jasper pushed through the group, hauling Joey and Alice along with them.

"We gotta be in the front row when they reach the wharf. After all, we were the first ones to see them," panted Izzie. *"Hurry!"* At last, they were standing in the deep snow close to the ladder.

There were three men in the boat. The children had never seen men look that tired, that wet, that *grim.* There were little icicles dribbling down from their woollen hats, and their faces looked blank and red, like polished apples. But the apples had whiskers on them, which were white with frost. They couldn't be fishermen. Fishermen wouldn't be out there on Christmas Day. A little shiver of fear crept up Izzie's spine.

When the boat arrived at the wharf, many hands reached down to help them up. Mr. Knickle even crept halfway down the slippery ladder to haul up the first man. They all climbed that ladder so slowly that you knew it was difficult for them to make their legs move.

Even though their clothes were sodden, it was clear that they were wearing uniforms. Izzie could see sailor collars under two of their coats. The third man had on a uniform she couldn't recognize. Maybe he was an officer.

When all three of them had reached the top of the wharf, everyone could tell how exhausted the men were, and how cold. But before the people could offer any help, one of the sailors began to speak. He spoke haltingly, and his words sounded as though he were speaking with his mouth full of dry bread.

"Two of us . . . are off a minesweeper . . . that went down . . . during the storm. We got adrift of our convoy . . . and a torpedo . . . grazed our rudder."

"And the other fella?" Mr. Hyson pointed at the third man, his head hunched down into his coat, shivering.

"He's a German," said the first sailor. "We picked him up . . . about half an hour after we sank . . . tossing around in a life jacket. Adrift from the sub . . . before she dove under."

Izzie could hear a murmur go up among the spectators on the wharf: "A German! The enemy!" A few people backed up, as though they were frightened. But some of the other men pushed forward, looking angry. The murmur turned into a roar.

Mr. Morash turned and faced the crowd. *"You can just quit that growling!"* he yelled. "Who do you think were some of the first settlers along this shore and in our own cove?" He paused for a moment, and then said, in a loud voice, "Germans!"

"Besides," said Mr. Hyson, whose great-great-grandfather had been German, "it's Christmas." He smiled over at Izzie—for the first time since she'd cut down his tree.

"And he's as frozen and tired as the others," added Mrs. Publicover, although she did look a bit nervous. After all, it was his submarine that had damaged the rudder on the minesweeper.

Izzie stepped forward. She faced the three bedraggled seamen and took in a deep breath. Standing very straight, she announced in a loud voice:

"I think you've been sent to us as a Christmas present. C'mon up to our house and get some warm clothes on. Then you can have a little nap. Right now we've got an extra bedroom. Because of old Uncle Herman. And in a few hours, you'll be our extra-special guests at the best Christmas party you've ever been to."

"And we needed guests very badly," added Jasper.

So that's what happened. The Morashes and Hysons and Knickles came over to the Publicovers' house with warm sweaters and pants and socks and extra blankets. Izzie made hot chocolate for the men, and Mrs. Publicover heated water from the well to let them wash. Then she put them to bed, each with a hot water bottle, under a big pile of blankets.

"Have a good sleep," called Izzie through the

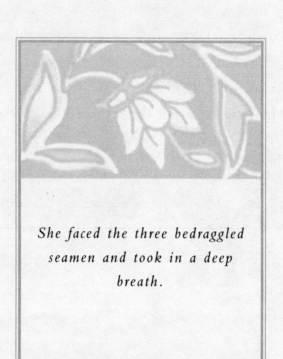

She faced the three bedraggled seamen and took in a deep breath.

bedroom doors. "We'll wake you up just before the party. You're gonna love it."

"Dinner's going to be very late," said Mrs. Publicover. "But it won't hurt any of us to be up half the night." She'd stopped thinking about the torpedo. After all, it was the storm that had sunk the minesweeper, not the submarine.

The Christmas party was something that Izzie would remember until she was an old, old woman. Over and over again, she would recall the scene as vividly as she was seeing it that evening. She would think back to the pink tablecloths laden with steaming turkeys, the homemade paper flowers, the candles and oil lamps flickering in the darkness, the tree full of birds and popcorn, the hot plum puddings with butter sauce. But most of all, she'd remember the faces of their three guests— whiskery, a little bit bleary-eyed, but full of amazed happiness. The German marvelled that some of the food came from old German recipes—pressed cucumbers with onions in sour cream, sauerkraut, a specially made local sausage—"Lunenburg pudding." But it was the turkey that the Canadian sailors loved best. Every so often one of them would doze off, only to wake up a moment later with a start and a big smile.

After the meal was cleared away, one of the sailors played old Uncle Herman's accordion, while Mrs. Publicover strummed her guitar. The other sailor taught Izzie and Jasper how to dance a foxtrot, and even Joey gave it a try. Izzie showed them how to do the South Shore polka—a great version with an extra stamp in it. The German—who was older than the other sailors and had two kids of his own—sat in Mrs. Publicover's rocking chair and held Alice, who had fallen asleep before they'd even got to the plum pudding. When everyone sang "Silent Night," he sang it in German, very softly: *"Stille Nacht . . ."*

When bedtime came—very late—the two Canadian sailors made their way over to sleep at the Morashes' house, because they had two extra mattresses in the attic. The German could have slept in old Uncle Herman's bed, but he chose to sleep on the couch in the Publicovers' kitchen, beside the warm wood stove. He'd stopped shivering a long time ago. He kept saying, *"Danke! Danke!"* which Izzie's father told her meant "Thank you. Thank you."

After they'd said goodnight to the seamen and the Morashes, the Publicovers put on their warm clothes and went outside to stand on the front deck of their house. Although it was after midnight, the snow looked white and mysterious under a bright moon. In front of them were the cove and the broad bay, shining smooth and peaceful in the still night.

"Flat-oil calm," said Mr. Publicover. "Old Mr. Gaetz was right again. You'll have another good coasting day tomorrow."

Then they all went into the house, stamped the

snow off their boots, hung up their outdoor clothes, and prepared for bed. Mr. Publicover blew out the candles and snuffed out the lamps—all except one, to light their way up the stairs.

Just before Izzie closed her eyes on the long day, she said to her parents and to Joey, "I know it maybe sounds awful to say this, but . . ."

"What?" asked her mother, as she tucked her in.

"Well, probably Grandpa and Grandma had a good Christmas anyway, with Aunt Julie in Yarmouth and all, and . . ."

"And?" Her mother was smiling.

"So, I really hope it's okay to say that this Christmas was . . ." She paused again.

Her mother finished her sentence for her: ". . . was absolutely the best one we've ever had."

"*Exactly!*" said Izzie, and fell asleep.

Glossary

Flat: A flat is a large rowboat (which is not flat-bottomed, like a dory). It has overlapping timbers along the sides (somewhat like clapboards on a house), and the oar locks consist of two wooden dowels, called thole pins. The oars fit between them. Flats are still used for bringing back fish—large and small—from the nets, and are often strung together in lines of 2 to 5, behind a motor boat. They are also used for manoeuvering around the huge net traps, from which the fish are "spilled" into the boats—the flats.

Launch: A launch is used for launching boats of various sizes (flats, dories, Cape Island motor boats), and for dragging them up beyond the high tide line for painting, repairing, and at times of big storms. It is usually made of pealed tree trunks. Launches lie flat, like enormous wide ladders, partly on the sea bottom, and partly on dry land.

Bark Pots: Bark pots used to be made of heavy metal—often cast iron—and held a heated solution of tar and hemlock bark, into which huge nets were immersed. The solution acted as a preservative. The nets were then dried before they were used again. As nylon nets and ropes became widely used, the "barking" of nets became less common.

Depth Charges: Depth charges were explosive devices used to disable or destroy submarines. They were released from the sterns of warships, and travelled downwards rather slowly through the water to their targets. They were awkward-looking weapons that resembled ordinary oil drums, but when they found their mark the results could be deadly.

Dear Reader,

Did you enjoy reading this Our Canadian Girl adventure? Write us and tell us what you think! We'd love to hear about your favourite parts, which characters you like best, and even whom else you'd like to see stories about. Maybe you'd like to read an adventure with one of Our Canadian Girls that happened in your hometown—fifty, a hundred years ago or more!

Send your letters to:

Our Canadian Girl
c/o Penguin Canada
10 Alcorn Avenue, Suite 300
Toronto, ON M4V 3B2

Be sure to check your bookstore for more books in the Our Canadian Girl series. There are some ready for you right now, and more are on their way.

We look forward to hearing from you!

Sincerely,

Barbara Berson
Penguin Books Canada

P.S. Don't forget to visit us online at www.ourcanadiangirl.ca—there are some other girls you should meet!

Canada's

1608
Samuel de Champlain establishes the first fortified trading post at Quebec.

1759
The British defeat the French in the Battle of the Plains of Abraham.

1812
The United States declares war against Canada.

1845
The expedition of Sir John Franklin to the Arctic ends when the ship is frozen in the pack ice; the fate of its crew remains a mystery.

1869
Louis Riel leads his Metis followers in the Red River Rebellion.

1871
British Columbia joins Canada.

1755
The British expel the entire French population of Acadia (today's Maritime provinces), sending them into exile.

1776
The 13 Colonies revolt against Britain, and the Loyalists flee to Canada.

1783
Rachel

1837
Calling for responsible government, the Patriotes, following Louis-Joseph Papineau, rebel in Lower Canada; William Lyon Mackenzie leads the uprising in Upper Canada.

1867
New Brunswick, Nova Scotia and the United Province of Canada come together in Confederation to form the Dominion of Canada.

1870
Manitoba joins Canada. The Northwest Territories become an official territory of Canada.

Timeline

1885
At Craigellachie, British Columbia, the last spike is driven to complete the building of the Canadian Pacific Railway.

1898
The Yukon Territory becomes an official territory of Canada.

1914
Britain declares war on Germany, and Canada, because of its ties to Britain, is at war too.

1918
As a result of the Wartime Elections Act, the women of Canada are given the right to vote in federal elections.

1945
World War II ends conclusively with the dropping of atomic bombs on Hiroshima and Nagasaki, Japan.

1873
Prince Edward Island joins Canada.

1896
Gold is discovered on Bonanza Creek, a tributary of the Klondike River.

1905
Alberta and Saskatchewan join Canada.

1917
In the Halifax harbour, two ships collide, causing an explosion that leaves more than 1,600 dead and 9,000 injured.

1939
Canada declares war on Germany seven days after war is declared by Britain and France.

1949
Newfoundland, under the leadership of Joey Smallwood, joins Canada.

1939
Ellen

1885
Marie-Claire

1941
Izzie

Check out the
Our Canadian Girl website

Fun Stuff

- E-cards
- Prizes
- Activities
- Poll

Fan Area

- Guest Book
- Photo Gallery
- Downloadable *Our Canadian Girl* Tea Party Kit

Features on the girls and more!

www.ourcanadiangirl.ca